D1145004

Have you seen my Potty?

by Mij Kelly and

Mary McQuillan

First published in 2007 by Hodder Children's Books

Text copyright © Mij Kelly 2007
Illustration copyright © Mary McQuillan 2007

Hodder Children's Books
338 Euston Road
London NW1 3BH

Hodder Children's Books Australia
Level 17/207 Kent Street
Sydney, NSW 2000

The right of Mij Kelly to be identified
as the author and Mary McQuillan as the illustrator
of this Work has been asserted by them in accordance
with the Copyright, Designs and Patents Act 1988.

All rights reserved

A catalogue record of this book is available
from the British Library.

ISBN: 978 0 340 91152 5
10 9 8 7 6 5 4 3 2 1

Printed in China

Hodder Children's Books
is a division of Hachette
Children's Books.

ROTHERHAM LIBRARY &
INFORMATION SERVICES

PB

B487563053

OES435294

To Joseph, Thomas and William – MK

For Amy and Jake, with love – MMcQ

Have you seen my Potty?

WRITTEN BY
MIJ
KELLY

ILLUSTRATED BY
MARY
McQUILLAN

Hodder
Children's
Books

A division of Hachette Children's Books

This is the story of Suzy Sue
who had something
very important to do,
something important
that she did every day…

...until someone

snatched her potty away.

What a terrible thing. What an awful to-do.
Who would play such a trick
on poor Suzy Sue?

Only a rascal quite ruthless
and rotten would steal
someone's potty from
under their bottom!

'Look what I found, lying around on the ground.'

'It's a pot.'
'It's a what?'

Oh what a disaster for poor Suzy Sue
who had something
very **important** to do.

'Have you seen my potty?'
she asked the cow.
But the cow didn't
want to talk right now.

'Besides, Suzy Sue,'
the cow pointed out,
'I've no idea
what
you're talking
about!'

'What's a potty?'
'I've no idea.'

'Hurry up
with the
poo-pot,
we're
desperate
here.'

Dairy Express

A

'It's so easy to use.'

'No faffing, no fuss.'

'This poo-pot's a work of pure genius!'

Oh what a disaster for poor Suzy Sue
who had something
very **important** to do.

'Have you seen my potty?' she asked the horse,
who was busy just then, but said that of course
he'd not seen her potty.
He knew this because
he had no idea
what a potty was!

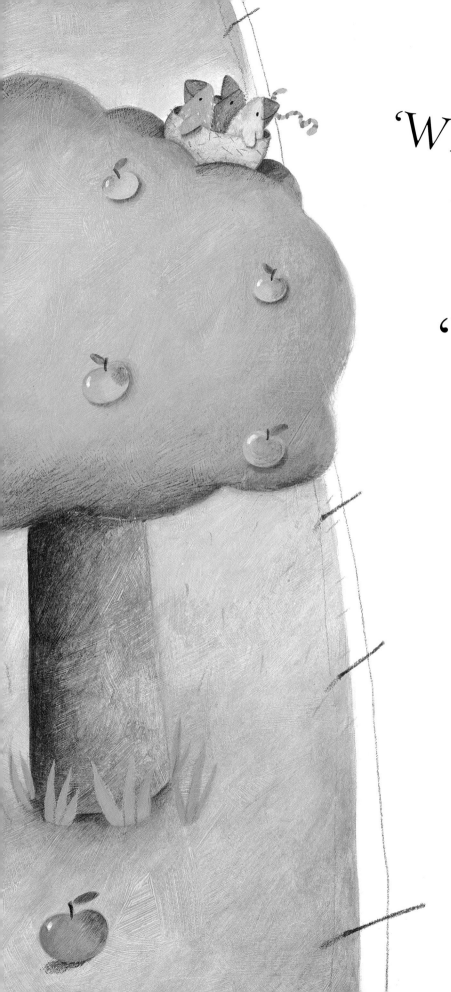

'What's a potty?'

'Don't ask me.'

'Hurry up with the poo-pot.'

'I need a wee.'

Oh what a disaster for poor Suzy Sue
who had something

very

important

to do.

'Have you seen my potty?' she asked the sheep,
who was perched on top
of a small red seat.

The sheep wanted to help.
He tried to look keen.
But this potty word,
oh what did it mean?

'What's the matter with Suzy Sue?'

'Don't ask me.'

'I need a poo!'

'What an **amazing** invention!'

'What a **wonderful** device!'

'A little **privacy** would be *nice*.'

Oh what a disaster for poor Suzy Sue
who had something

very important
to do.

'Have you
seen my
potty?'

she asked the goat,
who hummed and hawed
and cleared his throat.

'Beg pardon,' he said.
'Have I seen your wotty?
What is this thing
you call a potty?'

Oh what a disaster for poor Suzy Sue
who had something very **important** to do. . .

. . .something **important**
that she did **every** day.

If she couldn't find her potty…
she'd do it **anyway**.

'We've got the very thing for you.'

'Haven't you learnt...
or have you forgotten...
always poo with a poo-pot
under your bottom!'

That was the story of Suzy Sue
who had something
very important to do…